About the Illustrator

Name: ....

Age: .... Hometown: ....

One thing I'm really good at is: ....

The people and animals in my family include:

....

Some of my favorite things about my grandma are:

....

Grandma is a Superhero

COMPENDIUM®

kids™

inspiring possibilities.™

You wouldn't know it just by looking at her,

but my grandma is a superhero.

Like lots of grandmas,
she makes delicious cookies.

And she tells great stories, too.

But at night, she puts on her superhero costume and cape.

She does a few practice runs around the yard to warm up. And then, without even trying, she leaps up into the air.

She flies high up over the rooftops like a streak of color in the sky.

From far away, she sees a building that has caught on fire and zooms over to it. She hovers over the roof and shouts, "Rain cloud!"

A rain cloud appears and opens up, drenching the building

and putting out the fire before
the firefighters can even arrive.

When the firefighters come with their truck, Grandma has already finished the job.

They call out to her as she flies away: "We're lucky to have you, Super Grandma!"

Then, she's off in search of another adventure. *What's this? Grandma says to herself.* *A bunch of burglars trying to steal cakes from the bakery?* "Stop right there!" says Grandma.

Grandma makes them put the cakes back, and the burglars begin to cry.

They say they won't do it again.

And finally, Grandma has just enough time to rescue a >cat< from a treetop before the sun comes up.

In the morning, Grandma sips her coffee and says she's just a little tired today.

"You wouldn't believe what I did last night," she whispers to me with a wink.

WITH SPECIAL THANKS TO THE ENTIRE COMPENDIUM FAMILY.

CREDITS:

Written by: M.H. Clark
Designed by: Julie Flahiff
Edited by: Amelia Riedler

ISBN: 978-1-935414-94-0

3rd printing. Printed in China with soy inks. A011412003

COMPENDIUM®

kids™

inspiring possibilities.™